KAT MEREWETHER

Kuwi's Rowdy Crowd

Illustrated
PUBLISHING

Kuwi the Kiwi is relaxing
in her burrow.

Her chick, Huwi, is playing
quietly with his toys.

It is perfectly peaceful.

Kuwi makes herself a nice,
hot cup of kawakawa tea.

"Grrr! I'm Kiwi Kong!" hollers Huwi,
thumping around.

C-R-A-S-H,

clunk,

clash,

BUMP.

Kuwi sighs, and heads upstairs for a bubble bath.

She takes her hot cuppa with her.

Hovering Huwi follows.

Oh no! A flock of farting whio
are frolicking in the froth!

With every whio fluff,
Huwi laughs louder.

"Bobble blob blib
BLOB," hoots Huwi.

Kuwi shuffles into the quiet kitchen.
She sips her warm cuppa.

"Hiiiiiii-ya! Hiiiiiiiii-ya!"
Huwi cartwheels in with a
couple of karate-kicking kōkako.

"Hiiiiiiiiiiiii-YA!" hollers Huwi.

Kuwi silently scurries
to the spare room.

She sips her
heated-up cuppa.

"Mice mice baby. Mice mice baby."
Huwi rolls in with a rowdy rapping ruru.

"Mice mice BABY!" hip hops Huwi.

Kuwi tiptoes outside to
the tranquil terrace.

She sips her
lukewarm cuppa.

Tap tip tap tap tap.
Huwi is training with a
troupe of tap-dancing tomtits.

Tap tip tap tap TAP.
Huwi happily taps his toes.

Kuwi slowly steps to the
still and silent swamp.

She sips her cooling cuppa.

"Kihikihi kihikihi."
Huwi stampedes in with a singing swarm of cicadas.

"Kihikihi kihikihi!"
Huwi shrills in sync.

Kuwi patters off to the placid pond.

She sips her clammy cuppa.

Whack plup-plop.

Huwi is playing with a pair
of poo-pitching pekapeka.

Whack plup-PLOP!

Huwi pops the perfect pellet.

BAT
POO

Kuwi sneaks back
to the burrow.

She sips her chilly cuppa.

Bum brumm bum brumm bum.
Huwi bounds over with a brass band
of buzzing beetles.

Bum brum bum brum TISHH!
Huwi crashes two cymbals.

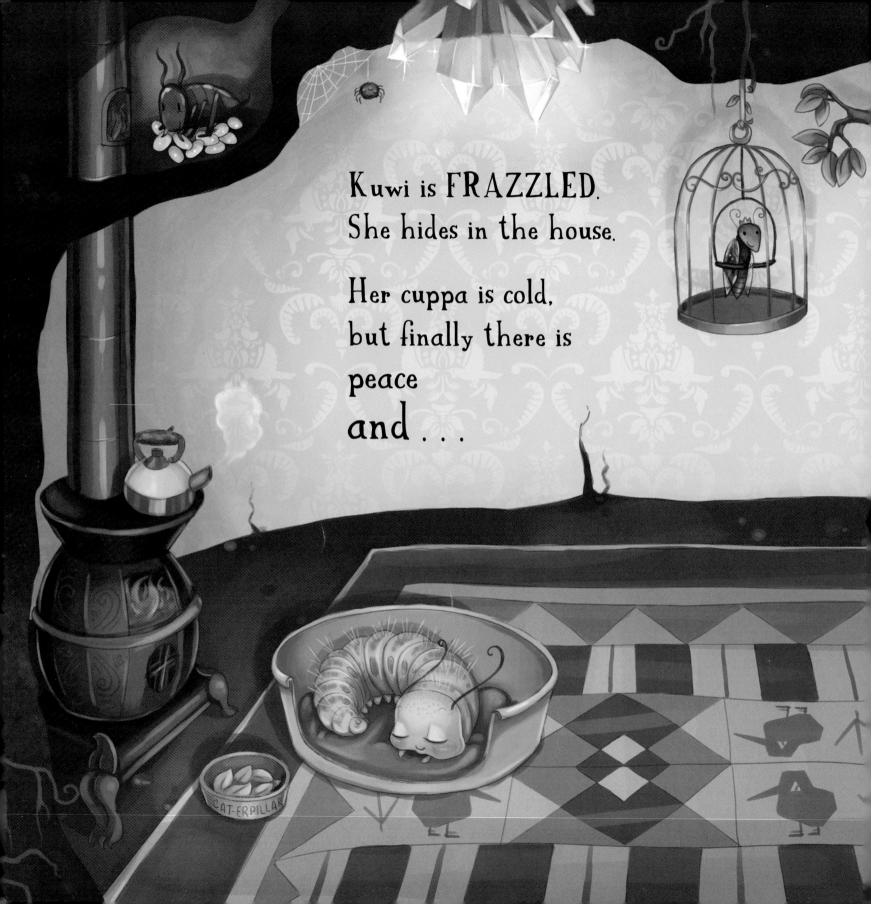

Kuwi is FRAZZLED.
She hides in the house.

Her cuppa is cold,
but finally there is

peace

and . . .

Bobble blob blob,
hiii-ya,
mice mice baby,
tap tip tap,
kihikihi kihikihi,
whack plup-plop,
bum brumm...

TISHH!

"QUIET!"
Kuwi cries.

The rowdy crowd slinks away.

Huwi cautiously and quietly
goes back to his toys.

He's careful not to make a sound.

Ahhhhhhh.
Finally. No more noxious noise.
The burrow is quiet.

Quiet . . .
and quite boring.

All the happy sounds have gone.
Kuwi is missing the noise.

Sincere thanks to my editors and advisors - Sue Copsey and Pānia Papa, for your knowledge and expertise.

First published in 2018 by Illustrated Publishing
P.O.Box 117, Te Awamutu 3840, New Zealand, Aotearoa

A catalogue record for this book is available from the National Library of New Zealand.

ISBN: 978-0-9941364-5-9

For more about this book and other titles visit www.illustrated.co.nz

Crash,

clunk,

clash,

B
  U
    M
      P.

For my delightfully deafening daughters,
Opal, Willow and Florence.

HOW TO SAY . . .

Kuwi - *koo-wee*

Huwi - *hoo-wee*

whio - *fee-aw*

kōkako - *kor-kuck-aw*

kihikihi - *key-he-key-he*

Te reo Māori / English

te reo Māori - native language of New Zealand

aroha - love

kawakawa - pepper tree

whio - blue duck

ruru - morepork

kihikihi - cicada

pekapeka - bat